Sleeping

RETOLD BY RUTH MATTISON • ILLUSTRATED BY ANN CARANCI

PIONEER VALLEY EDUCATIONAL PRESS, INC.

Once there was a king and a queen, who were very sad because they had no children. One day while the queen was sitting by a pond, a frog hopped out of the water.

The frog said, "Your wish will soon come true, and you will have a lovely daughter."

3

The frog's promise came true, and the king and queen had a beautiful little girl. They were happy and held a great celebration. They invited the fairies that lived in their kingdom. There were thirteen fairies in all, but because the king and queen had only twelve golden plates, one fairy was not invited.

The twelve fairies came to the celebration. Each one brought a magical present for the princess.

5

Just as the twelfth fairy was about
to give the princess her present,
the thirteenth fairy stormed in.
She was very angry that she had not
been invited. "On your daughter's
fifteenth birthday, she will prick
her finger on a spindle and fall
over dead," the thirteenth fairy told
the king and queen.

The king and queen were
very frightened. But the twelfth fairy
said, "It shall not be her death. My gift
will be that she will only fall into a
hundred-year sleep."

The king proclaimed
that all spindles in the entire
kingdom be burned.

Fifteen years passed. One day
the princess decided to explore the castle.

She came to some stairs
leading up to an old tower. She climbed
up the stairs and came to a small door.

She opened the door and saw
an old woman spinning wool.
"May I try spinning?"
she asked the old woman.

The princess touched the spindle
and pricked her finger.

At that very moment, she fell into
a deep sleep, and the king,
queen, and everyone who lived
in the castle began to fall asleep, too.

The horses in the stalls, the pigeons on the roof, the dogs in the courtyard, and the flies on the walls, all went to sleep. A prickly thorn hedge grew up around the entire castle, growing higher and higher, until nothing at all could be seen.

Many young princes heard about
the beautiful, sleeping princess and tried
to free her. No one could get through
the thorn hedge.

One hundred years passed.
A prince was traveling through the land
and heard an old man talking
about a beautiful princess asleep
in the castle behind the thorn hedge.

The old man said, "My grandfather told me stories about many princes who tried to get through the thorn hedge. But all who tried got stuck in the thorns and died a painful death.

"I am not afraid! I shall get through the hedge and free the beautiful princess," declared the prince.

13

When the prince came
to the thorn hedge, it turned
into flowers. He had no trouble,
and he walked right through.

The prince went into the castle.
He could see horses and dogs asleep
in the courtyard. Pigeons were sleeping
on the roof. He saw the flies sleeping
on the wall. He saw the cook
and the maids all asleep in the kitchen
and the hall. Everyone in the castle
was asleep.

The prince climbed up
to the old tower where the princess
was asleep. He bent over
and kissed her. She magically woke up.
The king, the queen, the cook,
the maids, the horses, and the dogs
woke up. The pigeons on the roof
and the flies on the walls woke up
as well.

The prince and princess got married
and lived happily ever after.